To Robert.
lots of

Atlanti

IRELAND
Dublin
Irish Sea

This book was published with the assistance of special grants from the Multiculturalism Program, Government of Canada, and the *Whig-Standard*, Kingston; and with the continuing support of the Canada Council and the Ontario Arts Council.

Design: Michael Solomon

Canadian Cataloguing in Publication Data

McSweeney, Susanne, 1943 –
The yellow flag

(Northern lights)

ISBN 0-88778-204-3 bd.

1. Irish in Canada – Juvenile fiction. 2. Quebec (Province) – History – 1791-1841 – Juvenile fiction.*
I. Clark, Brenda. II. Title. III. Series.

PS8575.S83Y44 JC813'.54 C80-094497-6
PZ7.M32Ye

Manufactured in Canada by Metropole Litho Inc.

PETER MARTIN ASSOCIATES LIMITED
280 Bloor Street West, Toronto, Canada M5S 1W1

The Yellow Flag

BY Susanne McSweeney

ILLUSTRATED BY Brenda Clark

Northern Lights

PUBLISHED BY PMA BOOKS

The letter from Canada made Mother's eyes shine with excitement. "Look, Brigid! Your father has sent the money for our passage to Quebec."

It was more than a year ago that Father had left Ireland to find work. With ten other strong men from our parish he was hired to dig a canal in Upper Canada. At last he had saved enough to pay our three fares across the ocean.

Lucy, my little sister, said it was hard to remember what father looked like. It was easier for me because I was already seven when he left. Besides, with her red hair and freckles, Lucy always reminded me of Father.

Mother and I both had thick black hair, and we never looked quite as cheery as Lucy, even

on her grumpy days.

"Thank the Lord we can leave now," said Mother. "The landlord has been after our land to graze his cattle. He said he would soon be sending his men to strip the thatch from our roof and tear all the turf from the walls. The money has come just in time!"

The next day before dawn we climbed onto Mr. O'Neil's cart for the ride into Dublin. Dublin was the city where he sold his livestock and where the ocean ships docked.

Lucy and I were wearing our only good dresses. We kept as far away from Mr. O'Neil's pigs as we could. The cart ride was bumpy and slow, and we were soon sore from the bouncing.

Then all at once such a salty breeze came up that we couldn't smell the pigs any more. We were nearing the Irish Sea. And way far ahead I could just make out little creatures jumping on spider webs.

"Those are sailors, Brigid, tying sails in our ship's rigging." Mother had never been to sea herself, but she remembered everything Father had written about the voyage.

What a crowd was at the Dublin docks! There were lots of children waiting to board our ship. We played hide and seek around the barrels until they were rolled onto the ship.

"Look out there, fellows! Put away your pipes!" shouted a sailor. "There's gunpowder in those barrels. Last week a ship blew up right here in the harbour because some fool was careless with a lighted pipe."

That scared me. I thought that all those barrels were full of food.

Mother grabbed Lucy's hand while I dragged our sack of clothes onto the ship, then down a hatchway into a long dark hall.

So this was the steerage! There must have been a hundred bunks, all squeezed together. There was just one bunk for the three of us. It was worse than our damp old cottage.

But on deck it was different. When we left the harbour and all the sails blew out in the wind, the ship looked tall and glorious. The bright blue sky peeked out between the puffed white sails like a checkerboard.

Alone for a moment I spread out my skirts to catch the breeze and be hustled along the deck.

"You look like a silly goose who can't fly," laughed my spying sister. I chased her back into the steerage.

After their work was done, some of the sailors talked and played with us, but others were mean and wouldn't let us come up on deck. When the crew had drunk a lot of rum we didn't dare go near *any* of them.

I suppose the captain was busy piloting the ship, because we never once saw him.

Lucy kept watching the sea for a sight of Canada, but the sailors only laughed.

"The Atlantic Ocean isn't the little Irish Sea," they told her. "It will take weeks to cross it, and with the calm days we're having, maybe months."

Then one night, when we were in the middle of the ocean and only half way to Canada, a horrible howling storm came up. Water began leaking down into the steerage as heavy waves crashed over the deck.

Mother tied us to our berth to keep us from being thrown about and bruised. The babies were screaming and some of my friends were crying.

"Let us all pray," said Father Kelly, "and ask God to save our lives."

Later we sang hymns, louder and louder to cover the noise of the wind—all night, until the storm blew itself out.

The voyage was too long to be fun any more. Most days were very dull. Every morning we had potatoes or oatmeal, and the same at noon, and the same at night.

Our food tasted stale, and sometimes it had black beetles in it. The water was so scummy we hated to drink it.

Lucy grew skinnier than ever. Her red hair looked brown, it was so dirty. I think we both had lice on our heads.

Some of the passengers looked worse than we did. One old woman seemed very sick. She kept screaming for water.

Mother called out for the ship's surgeon. He

brought water to the old woman, and he made a cut in her arm to let out the bad blood.

My mother wept when she heard the woman had cholera. "It's a terrible, dangerous disease. It starts with a fever and then it seems to strangle your stomach. In Dublin hundreds of people died from it."

Early the next day Lucy and I heard a bell clanging slowly. Then we saw the priest making the Sign of the Cross over three bodies as they were wrapped in sheets and tipped into the ocean.

I was so tired of the sea! We had been sailing for almost two months and still had not reached Canada.

Then one day my sister came running down from the deck. “Brigid, Brigid!” she cried. “There’s a huge white mountain sitting in the water, all by itself!”

We saw another one and then another.

“Those must be icebergs,” Mother said. “Just one more day and I think we’ll see land.”

Everyone cheered and started talking about the good things to come in Canada.

"I'm going to build myself a cottage," one man said, "that no landlord will ever take away from me." "We'll finally have enough food to eat," said another, "something besides potatoes."

I was hoping Father's work on the Rideau Canal was almost finished. Maybe he would take us to fish or even swim in it.

After we sailed past the icebergs a thick cold fog settled around the ship.

"This is a dangerous place," a sailor said quietly to Mother. "We're very near the coast of Newfoundland where many ships have been wrecked on the rocks."

By the time the fog cleared, the captain had steered us away from the rocks. We had sailed past Nova Scotia and New Brunswick. We were entering the great Saint Lawrence River!

For two days we sailed up the river towards Quebec City. Then just off the shore of a small island our ship dropped anchor.

"Where are we, Mother? This can't be Quebec!"

"No," she said wearily. "This is Grosse Isle, the quarantine island."

We heard a shout from the captain: "Run up the yellow flag!"

Nobody cheered that flag. It meant there was cholera on board. Only a doctor could come near us.

"This ship is filthy!" said the doctor when he came aboard. He ordered the crew to scrub the deck and the passengers to clean out the steerage.

Now that we had fresh water we could wash our clothes and hang them to dry in the rigging. The women took the bedding and pounded it clean on the shore.

But Mother did not try to help. She was very pale and her hands shook. She was too weak to move from our berth.

"Brigid," she whispered, "take good care of

your sister. Promise me you will."

When the doctor came to examine the passengers he said Mother had cholera and would have to be carried to his hospital sheds on the island.

"She will need our help for a while. But you two must stay healthy and wait for her in Quebec City."

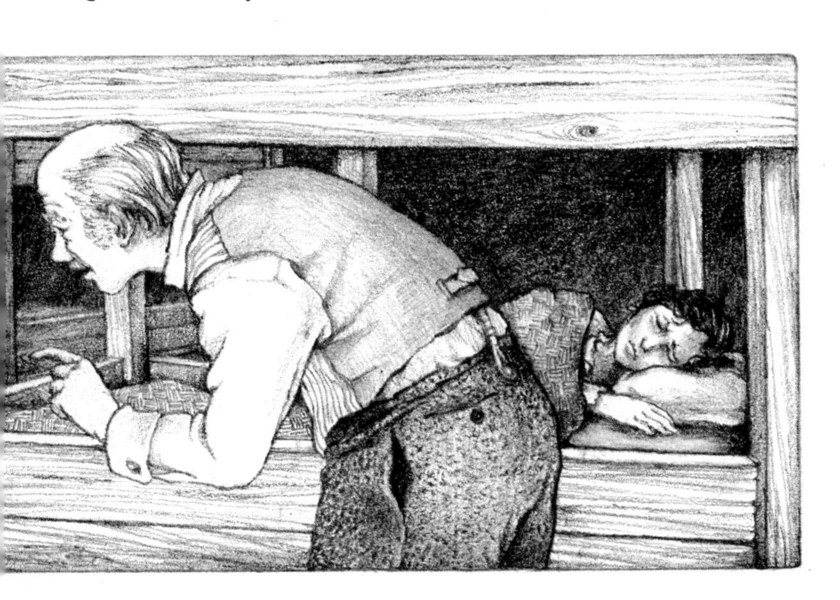

There was nothing else for us to do. We were scared for Mother and for ourselves. How could we get along without her? I wished we had never left Ireland, even if we had always been hungry there.

When we docked at Quebec we heard bells tolling for the dead. Lucy started crying. She wanted Mother.

We were hungry, but when I asked people on the docks for help, they turned away. One lady was carrying some loaves of bread. She smiled and gave me a loaf, then hurried past. Did we look so awful?

At last we heard a cheerful voice—"Ah, children, I have been hours searching for you!" It was Father Kelly, the priest from our ship. "I want you to stay with my old friend Madame Chaperon in the Upper Town of Quebec City. She can speak some English and she knows that you do not have cholera. Most people here are blaming the Irish ships for bringing this plague to Canada."

So that was why no one would help us.

All that summer we lived in a tall, grey stone house with Madame Chaperon. She fed us until even Lucy was plump.

Every day she took us to Mass to pray for our mother.

Sometimes we saw coffins being pulled

through the streets. There were more and more graves marked with crosses.

I was afraid that we might never see Mother again. Would one of those graves be hers? I never said this to Lucy.

Then, just before the river froze, a boat arrived from Grosse Isle. Lucy and I raced down the hill to meet it.

And there was Mother standing on deck! She must have heard our voices for she looked very

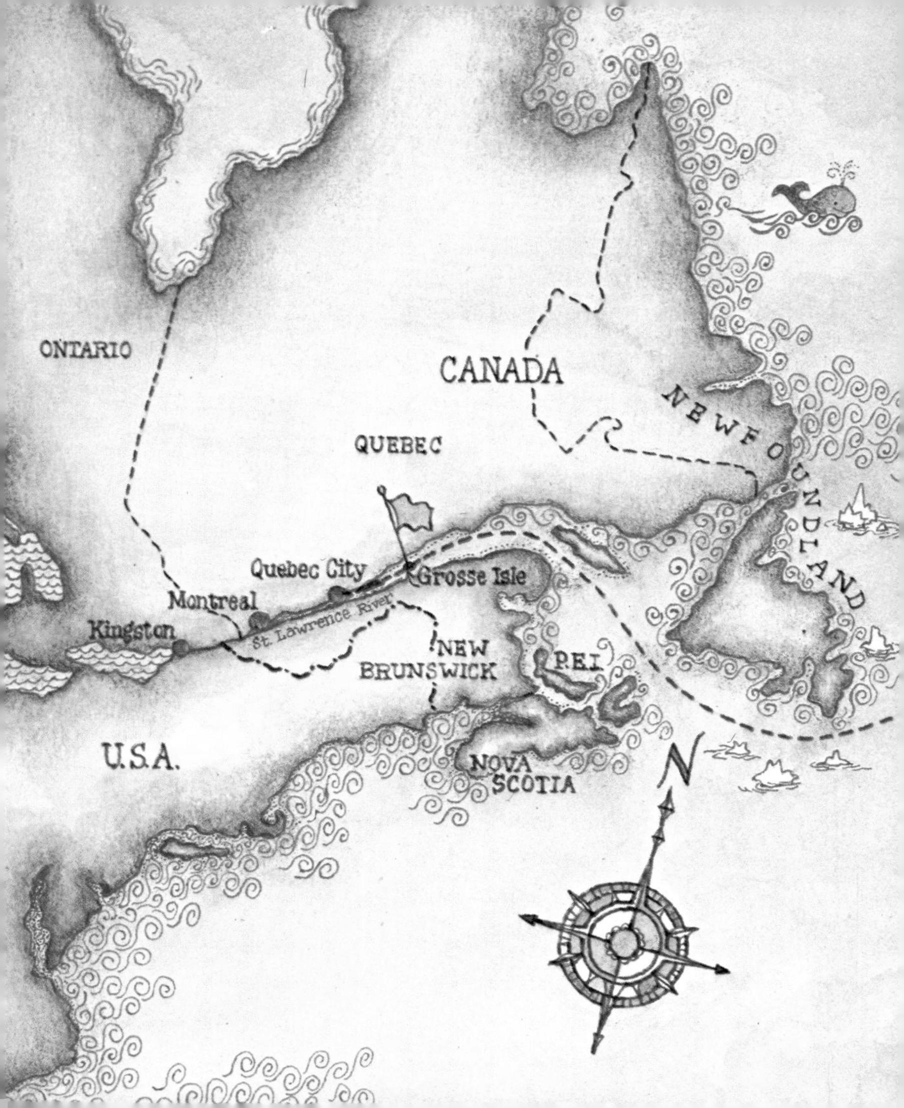
ONTARIO
CANADA
QUEBEC
NEWFOUNDLAND
Quebec City
Grosse Isle
Montreal
Kingston
St. Lawrence River
NEW
BRUNSWICK
P.E.I.
U.S.A.
NOVA
SCOTIA
N

OTHER *Northern Lights* BOOKS

The Last Ship
by Mary Alice Downie
illustrated by Lissa Calvert

Madeleine and twin brother Charles battle a fire in 17th-century Quebec City the eve before the last ship of the season leaves for France.

Streets of Gold
by George Rawlyk
illustrated by Leoung O'Young

Thirteen-year-old Jonathan Barble lies about his age to join the New England forces in their assault on the French fortress at Louisbourg.

The Sky Caribou
by Mary Hamilton
illustrated by Debi Perna

Chipewyan Little Partridge entrusts his friend Samuel Hearne with an important mission as the great explorer sets off for the legendary copper fields at Coppermine River.

The Buffalo Hunt
by Donald and Eleanor Swainson
illustrated by James Tughan

Pierre is rescued from the path of a charging buffalo during his first ride in the great Métis fall buffalo hunt.

Michi's New Year
by Shelley Tanaka
illustrated by Ron Berg

Michi finds life in Vancouver strange and lonely, but a Japanese New Year's party brightens her spirits.

Then we started out on the last part of our long journey, up the Saint Lawrence to Kingston and our father.

happy. We threw our arms around her and could hardly see through our tears. How good it was to be with her again!

We stayed in Quebec until Mother was strong enough for the rest of the journey. We would go first to Montreal and then to Kingston.

We could not travel by steamboat because the river was almost all ice. "I hate boats now anyway," said Lucy.

"We'll be like real Canadians!" Mother told us. "We shall take a stage coach with runners that horses can pull over the frozen roads and even on the river itself."

Madame Chaperon gave us a bearskin rug to keep us warm in the coach. Mother promised to write her all about our new home. What a kind woman she was, our first Canadian friend.